One Golden Year

A STORY OF A GOLDEN RETRIEVER

Look for these books (and more)
in the Dog Tales series:

One Golden Year

The Westie Winter

DOG TALES #1

One Golden Year

A STORY OF A GOLDEN RETRIEVER

BY COLEEN HUBBARD

Illustrations by Lori Savastano

AN
APPLE
PAPERBACK

SCHOLASTIC

New York   Toronto   London   Auckland   Sydney

For Susie Davis,
real-life puppy raiser,

and

Jim Hunt,
who made the connection.

ISBN 0-590-18975-1

12 11 10 9 8 7 6 5 4 3 2 1   8 9/9 0 1 2 3/0

Printed in the U.S.A.   40
First Scholastic printing, October 1998

CONTENTS

ONE

Albion Arrives

"I can't wait to see him!" said Caitlin Connor as she paced the linoleum floor of the airport cargo office. "The newest member of our family!"

"It's sort of like waiting to see your new baby," observed Kath, her mom. "You have no idea what you're in for."

"At least," said Caitlin, "we know he won't have Will's hair color." She reached over and ruffled her eight-year-old brother's hair, which was a bright orange-red, passed down from their grandfather. Though he hated being called "carrottop" and "pumpkin head," Caitlin knew that Will was actually very proud of his distinctive hair.

Will rolled his eyes at his eleven-year-old sister, whose long brown hair and green eyes exactly matched their mother's. "Everyone knows golden retrievers have *gold* hair. Otherwise they'd be called red retrievers, or brown retrievers, or purple retrievers, or —"

"Okay," interrupted Caitlin. "We get your point."

"And just like a baby," continued their mom, "we'll love this puppy no matter what he looks like."

"Yeah." Caitlin sighed, twisting the ends of her ponytail. "We'll love him, raise him, and train him. And then in a year we'll just give him up and say good-bye. We must be crazy to be doing this!"

"I can't think of a better thing for us to do this year," said Kath. "It will distract us from missing Dad so much, and since I'm taking a year off from work, I'll have lots of time to devote to the dog."

"While you're on your radical," Will added.

"My what?" Kath asked, confused.

"He means your *sabbatical*," Caitlin explained. "Your time off." Kath was taking a year off from the high school she had taught at for the past decade. Both Will and Caitlin were looking forward to having her home more.

"Well, I almost said it right," Will protested, dribbling an imaginary soccer ball on the slippery floor.

"But mostly you want to do this because of Mrs. Storbel, right?" asked Caitlin. Linda Storbel taught Spanish at West High with Kath, and over the years the two had become close friends.

"Right," Kath agreed. "When Mrs. Storbel was first confined to her wheelchair, she didn't think she could continue teaching. And then she got her assistance dog and it changed her life. Oz opens doors for her, picks up papers, holds her briefcase. And if someone hadn't raised Oz for his first year and loved him, he would never have become Mrs. Storbel's companion."

"You're right," said Caitlin, "but still —"

Just then, a man in a blue uniform brought over a small white travel kennel and set it on the floor in front of them. "Are you the Connors?" he asked.

"That's us!" Will shouted.

"Then this animal is for you," said the man, handing Kath a long pink form to sign.

Before her mom could even pick up the pen, Caitlin was on her knees, unlatching the wire door. Then she reached inside and brought out the sleepy, curled-up puppy.

"Oh, Albion," she said, cuddling the dog to her chest. "You are the most adorable puppy in the whole world."

"Look!" said Will, grabbing his mother's arm. "Look! Albion *does* have reddish hair. His coat is reddish gold!"

Gently, Caitlin held Albion up so her mom and brother could see him better. Besides his soft, golden coat, he had a black nose, dark eyes, and furry ears that hung down to his jaw. His legs were solid and strong, and his small puppy tail wagged back and forth.

"He looks as if he's smiling," said Kath, noticing the way his mouth turned up at the corners.

"Oh, look!" Caitlin said, pointing to the under-

side of Albion's ear. "There's his tattoo — the one that shows he belongs to Canine Family."

Will and Kath examined the tiny marking, which bore a number and logo. It made Caitlin feel good to know that if anything ever happened to the dog, he could be easily identified.

"Cute dog," said the uniformed man as he tore off a copy of the pink form. "Where'd he come from?"

Caitlin started to answer, but when she looked up at the man, she froze. She hated how shy she always became around people she didn't know.

"Tell him about Albion," her mother urged. "You're going to have to get used to answering questions about him. For the next year, Albion will go everywhere we go."

Caitlin looked at her mother and shrugged helplessly. Then she pulled Albion closer and buried her face in his thick fur.

"Well," said Will, happily taking over, "I'll tell you. He was born in California and his parents are special breeding dogs from Canine Family. We're going to raise him for a year and then he'll go back to California to a special school."

"You don't say?" asked the man.

Will continued, hardly taking a breath. "Then someone in a wheelchair will get him for a companion. And my mom and my sister are called puppy raisers, and my sister even has a special card in her wallet that says that even though she's a kid, she's been certified to be a puppy raiser. She filled out a lot of papers and had to be interviewed by the dog trainer."

"Well, good for them," said the man, reaching over to pat the puppy. "How'd he get the name Albion, anyway?"

Will shook his head and looked over at his mom.

"Canine Family dogs are often named for people who support the organization," Kath answered. "Apparently, a woman named Mrs. Albion loves animals very much and believes in the idea of assistance dogs."

"Well," said the man as he moved back to the counter, "good luck to all of you."

Caitlin kept her face buried, breathing in Albion's earthy but sweet puppy smell. *If only I were outgoing like Will,* she thought. *I always seem like such an idiot.*

Albion gave Caitlin's cheek a quick, wet lick. She laughed, and suddenly realized that she loved him already.

"I think we should call him Alby," Caitlin announced.

To Caitlin, the half-hour drive home from the airport seemed to take forever. But they finally arrived at the Connors' two-story redbrick house. After sleeping in his travel kennel all the way home, Alby was eager to explore his new surroundings. He became instantly alert and excited, sniffing every corner of every room.

"Let's show him where he's going to sleep," said Will, bounding up the stairs to their mother's room. "You're going to sleep here, next to Mom, so she can keep an eye on you."

"Right," said Caitlin. "Here's your own special crate." She showed Alby the large wire crate spread with a cozy blanket.

"Why is *that* thing in the crate?" asked Will, pointing to the red plastic picnic cooler pushed against the back.

"To create a smaller space for him while he's a puppy," Caitlin explained. "We'll take it out when he's bigger."

"Let's show him the backyard," said Will, who was almost as excited as the puppy. "I want him to see the fort I'm building."

"Slow down," said Caitlin. "I'm out of breath."

On the way out of her mother's room, Caitlin stopped to pick up a framed picture of her father from the dresser. He was wearing a blue denim shirt and a baseball cap, and giving the camera his usual half-crooked smile.

"Alby, this is our dad," Caitlin explained, holding the picture in front of the puppy's face. "His name is Ned. He's working in Ohio for a whole year, supervising a huge hospital that his company is building. So, unfortunately, you're not going to be seeing him very often."

"Practically never," Will complained, trying to sound tough instead of sad. "Like maybe once a month."

"He can't help it," Caitlin said. "He has to go where the work is."

"You sound like Mom," Will teased. "Miss Junior Grown-up!"

"Oh, go eat a peanut," Caitlin responded.

Will had a mild allergy to peanuts, which was annoying but not really dangerous. It was the perfect thing to tease Will about whenever Caitlin wanted to get even!

Still holding Alby, Caitlin looked out the bedroom window. A girl with short, sandy-colored hair rode by on her bike, followed by several other girls. The girls were laughing and talking, clearly having a wonderful time.

"Alby, that's Shawna," Caitlin explained. "She

lives down the street from us, but you'll probably never meet her. I've never had the guts to talk to her at school, and she and her friends certainly ignore me."

Just then the doorbell rang. Alby squirmed and tried to escape from Caitlin's arms. He barked a high-pitched puppy bark, his ears twitching toward the sound.

"It's probably Kevin and Alex," said Will. "I told all my friends to come over and meet Albion."

"I think he's supposed to have a quiet first day," Caitlin reminded her brother, heading for the stairs. "Not be surrounded by all your gooney friends."

"Yes, sir! Miss Dog Trainer, sir!" Will teased, giving his sister an exaggerated salute.

"Caitlin!" called their mother from downstairs. "Regina is here!"

Regina Davis was an experienced trainer from Canine Family. She was one of the people who had interviewed Caitlin and her mom when they first applied to become puppy raisers. She would be working closely with the Connors and Albion during the coming year.

"Hi, Regina!" Caitlin called, coming down the stairs with Alby in her arms. "He's here!"

"So I see!" Regina laughed, reaching over to pet the dog. "How's he doing?" Regina was tall, with short blonde hair, and a deep, rich voice that easily captured the attention of anyone within range — dogs as well as people.

"Well, aside from disappearing under the bed, fine."

"He's trying to get to know his new home," Regina explained. Her arms were filled with books and she carried a neon-yellow bag. "How about if we let your brother take him outside while I talk to you and your mom?"

"Great!" said Will, taking the puppy from Caitlin. "I want to show you my fort," he said to Albion as he headed for the back door. "I started it with my dad and it's going to be really cool! It's made out of wood — wait until you see it."

"Make sure the gate's closed," Kath called after him as she sat down in a rocking chair by the fireplace.

"I have lots of goodies for you," Regina began, reaching into her yellow bag. "I have the training manual and a few basic books on dog behavior. And I have Albion's cape, plus the fanny pack for you and your mom."

Caitlin took the tiny yellow cloth cape printed with the name and logo of Canine Family. Albion would wear the cape whenever he was in public, so that people could recognize him as an assistance dog in training.

"Remember," continued Regina, "you need to wear the fanny pack whenever you take Albion out with you. It's a good place to store puppy treats, business cards for our organization, and a copy of the state law that allows Albion to enter public places. Believe me, you'll need that."

"Why?" asked Caitlin.

"Because not many people realize that our state passed this law, and you'll probably have to remind folks about it when you take Alby into stores and restaurants," explained Regina.

"Do all fifty states have the same law?" Kath asked.

Regina shook her head sadly. "Unfortunately not. In fact, our state is one of the few. That's why we have such a strong puppy-raiser program here."

"When is the first training class?" Caitlin asked.

"You should start in two weeks. Tuesday nights at the rec center at six P.M."

"I'm nervous," said Caitlin. "I'm afraid we'll do something wrong before then."

"Don't be nervous," Regina replied. "All you have to do right now is love Albion and help him get used to your home. And keep him safe and healthy, of course. The rest you'll learn as we go along."

"And what about the puppy scrapbook?" asked Kath. "Are we supposed to start that now?"

"Yes," Regina replied. "Your record of Albion's first year will be very meaningful to the person Albion eventually works with. Pictures, written notes — whatever you want to include."

"It's like a baby book," said Kath. "Like the records I kept of you and Will when you were young."

"Exactly," said Regina.

"I've already bought a scrapbook," said Caitlin. "And about ten rolls of film."

"And, Caitlin, it's not too early to start thinking ahead to the time when you'll have to give Albion back to Canine Family. As much as you may grow to love him, you have to remember that he's not a family pet."

Caitlin was startled by Regina's words. They sounded so cold and harsh. And the truth was, Caitlin didn't want to start thinking about that day, a long time from now. For now, Alby was hers.

They had all the time in the world.

Alby's Puppy Book

September 8th

Today Albion arrived at the airport. We decided right away to call him Alby. My dad always says that nicknames mean you love that person — or dog, in this case! I'm including the form we signed for Alby's release, just as a souvenir. He'll be sleeping in my mom's room in a special dog crate. It's made of metal wire, so you can see through it and he'll get lots of fresh air — but he won't be able to wander around at night and get in trouble! We also bought him a squeaky doughnut to chew on. Our first big job is to begin teaching him to go to the bathroom outside. Since I've never had a dog before, I'm not exactly sure how to do this, but our trainer gave us some books to read. We have a lot of appointments scheduled at the vet for shots, checkups, etc. We have to make sure Alby stays healthy and gets the right food and exercise. I took some pictures of him exploring our house, and as soon as they're developed, I'll paste them in this book. Then you'll be able to see that he's the cutest puppy in the world. He always looks like he's smiling, and his tail never stops wagging!

TWO

The First Puppy Class

"Alby, I'm home!" Caitlin shouted.

She slammed the front door behind her and ran into the family room. Her mom was sitting at the computer, paying bills.

"Where's Alby?" Caitlin asked, dropping her backpack and jacket on the floor.

"Gee," teased her mom. "You used to say hello to *me* after school. Now you just want to talk to the dog!"

Alby emerged from underneath the computer desk, wagging his tail and hurrying over to sniff Caitlin's sneakers. He took the shoelace from her left shoe between his teeth and began to pull. Caitlin plopped down on the floor and scooped him up in her arms, interrupting his game of tug-of-war.

"Hey, Alby! I don't think I'm supposed to let you do that. Where's your chew toy?"

"Right here," said Kath, handing Caitlin a yellow plastic squeaky toy shaped like a doughnut. "Chew on this, Alby."

But Alby was only interested in Caitlin. He curled up in her lap and licked her hand. His tail wagged back and forth.

My favorite part of the day, Caitlin thought — *coming home to Alby!*

"How was school?" Kath asked, turning off the computer. "Are you making any new friends?"

"Not really," Caitlin answered. She petted the soft ruff of fur around Albion's neck. "But it's okay. Alby's my buddy, aren't you, Alby? Alby doesn't care if I'm shy."

Kath gave her daughter a worried look. But then she smiled as she watched Caitlin and Alby play with the squeaky doughnut.

"Don't forget," Kath reminded Caitlin, "tonight

is our first puppy-training class. We need to have an early dinner. And I'm having a baby-sitter come for Will. I don't think your brother will make it through a two-hour class."

Caitlin looked at Albion and then at her mother. "I hope no one will be able to tell that we've never had a dog before. I hope we don't look like total beginners."

"Well, we are beginners," her mom said with a laugh. "But I bet the three of us will do just fine."

At six o'clock sharp, Caitlin and Kath walked Alby through the front door of the neighborhood rec center. Alby wore his yellow cloth cape and a special leash (called a gentle lead) designed to fit over his nose. Caitlin wore the yellow fanny pack. It was filled with tiny dog treats, which would be used to reward Alby's good behavior.

"Oh, Caitlin," said Kath. "Look at all the dogs!"

Caitlin counted at least a dozen dogs and their raisers gathered in the large, open room. Ranging in age from a few months to just over a year, the group of yellow-caped dogs was a happy sight.

"This is heaven," sighed Caitlin. "A dozen puppies as cute as Alby."

While Kath went to speak to Regina, Caitlin noticed a boy about her age with an energetic black puppy. She knew it wasn't a retriever because of its color and short, stiff coat. To her surprise, the boy walked right over to her, a warm smile on his face. He was about Caitlin's height, with dark brown hair and wide, gray-green eyes.

"Hi," he said, grinning at Caitlin. "Do you think there's a secret puppy-raiser handshake or something?"

Caitlin blushed and managed to squeak out a hello.

"Nice dog," he said. "Golden, right?"

"Right," she answered, keeping her gaze on the boy's dog. She couldn't make herself look the boy in the eye, even though he seemed so friendly.

"Ours is a black Lab," he continued. "Regina

said that Canine Family only uses Labs, retrievers, or a mix of both."

"Really?" Caitlin responded, hoping she didn't sound too stupid. "Why is that?"

"Because of their breeding. Both breeds have the ability to learn all the commands they'll need to become assistance dogs. And also because they're friendly and love people."

"And they're loyal," added Caitlin, leaning over to give Alby's head a pat. "And smart."

"What's your name?" the boy asked.

"Albion," Caitlin answered. "I mean Caitlin! I mean — Alby is my dog and I'm Caitlin."

Though Caitlin felt she would die of embarrassment, the boy continued to smile at her, not seeming to notice how she had stumbled over her words.

"I'm Keith," he said. "And my dog is Bailey. It looks like we're the only kids in the class, so we'll have to stick together."

Caitlin liked Keith instantly. He was different

from the boys at school who acted tough all the time and wouldn't be caught dead talking to a girl. Still, she was glad when Regina called the class to order. Now she wouldn't have to think of what to say next.

But as Caitlin tried to pull Alby away from Bailey, the leashes of both dogs became completely entangled. Keith and Caitlin tugged and twisted until they were both laughing. But the puppies stayed stuck, sniffing and licking each other. And every time the happy dogs rolled around or jumped up on each other, they tangled the leashes even more!

"Don't worry," Regina told them. "Pretty soon you'll know what to do to avoid a puppy pile. It happens a lot in the beginning."

Finally, Alby and Bailey settled down. Caitlin stood expectantly next to her mom, ready to begin the first lesson.

Regina introduced the new puppy raisers and their dogs to the rest of the class. Some of the puppies had been in training for months already, and

several of the older dogs were almost ready to leave their raisers and move on to the advanced training in California.

Caitlin still couldn't make herself think about giving up Alby at the end of the year. She looked around and wondered how the other raisers could be so calm and happy when they knew what was coming.

I'm glad we're just beginning, Caitlin thought, glancing down at Alby.

"Today," began Regina, "I'm going to work first with the new puppies on taking food gently. We never want our dogs to be greedy or aggressive when taking treats from us. And we're going to work on training our dogs to never, never eat food off the ground."

"Why is that?" Caitlin asked. She surprised herself by asking the question without stopping to think about what to say.

"Good question," answered Regina. "When these puppies become assistance dogs, they will have very specific responsibilities to their humans.

They can't be distracted by food that might be lying around."

"What about table scraps?" asked another new
member of the class. "Can we ever feed our dogs
people food?"

"Never," answered Regina. "And that's very
important. These dogs need to expect to eat only
dog food, and to eat it only at specific times. They
can't beg for food — that's not part of their job.
And it's much healthier for your dogs to eat a diet
of high-quality dog food anyway."

"We'll have to explain all of this to Will," Kath
whispered to Caitlin. "No giving Alby the broccoli
and peas he doesn't want to eat!"

Then Regina demonstrated how to use dog
treats to reward the puppies when they made good
decisions about their behavior. "When you see
your dog do something right, reach down and give
a treat. Then say, 'Good girl!' or 'Good boy!' right
away."

Regina asked everyone in the class to practice
saying "good girl" and "good boy" in an enthusi-

astic voice. "Watch how the dogs wag their tails when you praise them with excited voices. When you say it in a quiet, bored voice it doesn't make the same impression."

Caitlin felt a little silly saying "good boy" over and over in a high-pitched, happy voice. But she could tell that Alby paid attention to her when she hit the right note.

"I'm tired," Caitlin said at the end of the class. "That's hard work."

"It is," her mother agreed. "We have a lot to learn. Next class we work on the 'sit' command."

"I want to sit right now," Caitlin said. "My legs are tired from standing."

"So are Alby's." Kath laughed. "Look at him."

Alby was fast asleep on the floor, his sweet face resting between his two front paws.

I love this dog, Caitlin thought. *Alby's my friend. And maybe Keith and Bailey will be my friends, too.*

Alby's Puppy Book

September 22nd

Tonight was Alby's first training class! He made his first canine friend — a black Lab named Bailey. I'll have to take a picture of the two of them so you'll be able to see him. It seems a little strange to be writing to a person I don't know, but my mom says it's just like keeping a baby book and that I should tell you all about Alby's "firsts" — the first time he does something exciting. Here's a first for you — I went to get the ironing board out of the hall closet to iron a shirt for school, and Alby was really afraid of it. He barked and backed away, and his hair stood up around his neck. We have to take time to let him smell every new thing he comes across. I'm learning that dogs have *forty* times the smell power that we humans have. And since retrievers were bred to hunt, their sense of smell has always been really strong. I tried an experiment with my brother. One of us would hide in a room of our house, and then the other would carry Alby to that room. *Every single time* he sniffed us out!

September 30th

We just got Alby's identification tag. I can't put it in the scrapbook, so I'm drawing a picture of it for you. It's blue with silver writing.

Alby totally loves his squeaky doughnut and carries it all over the house and yard. He acts like a kid with a favorite toy or blanket. He also has a favorite place to sleep during the day — under my mom's computer desk. It's warm down there, and he can smell my mom nearby.

October 15th

Alby just met my dad! His name is Ned and he's working in another state for a while. But he came home for the weekend and he and Alby had a great time. When my dad cleaned out the garage, Alby wouldn't leave him alone. He followed him all around, sniffing everything — like bike tires, garbage cans, and our old wading pool! My dad says he can tell there's something special about Alby from the way he pays such close attention to everything around him. Now my dad calls Alby "Detail Dog."

November 20th

It's almost Thanksgiving. While we eat turkey, Alby will just eat more puppy chow. I think it would be a very boring diet, but the trainers tell us that we can't give the dogs human food. So, no pumpkin pie for Alby. Oh, guess what? I've been getting together with Keith, from our training class, and his dog, Bailey. We practice commands and let the dogs socialize. Here's a picture of both puppies — one gold and one black.

THREE

Going Public

"Alby, we're going Christmas shopping!" said Caitlin. "It'll be your first trip to the mall."

Albion scampered over to Caitlin, his tail wagging. Whenever he saw his leash, he knew he was about to be taken out into the big world. Now that he was five months old, he went everywhere with the Connor family.

"Do you have your fanny pack?" Kath asked as she put on her coat. "We can't forget that."

"Got it," said Caitlin. She fastened the yellow pack loosely over her red-and-purple parka.

"Sit," Caitlin said to Alby. Alby quickly sat and looked up, ready for his praise. "Good boy!" she responded, reaching down to hand him a piece of puppy kibble.

"Now stay," Caitlin said.

Then she hooked Alby's yellow cape around his belly as he patiently waited in his stay position. Caitlin noticed how big he was getting — the cape barely fit him anymore. His face had lost that distinctive puppy look, and his paws seemed enormous.

"Isn't he good?" Caitlin asked her mother. "Don't you think Alby's the best dog in the whole world?"

"He's doing great," Kath agreed. "And so are you. I'm really proud of how responsible you've been with him."

"Thanks." Caitlin laughed. "Maybe you should pat me on the head and say, 'Good girl!' "

"And give you a puppy treat to chew on!"

"Yuck!" Caitlin shuddered. "You have to be a dog to like those things."

But it made Caitlin happy to know that she was handling her puppy-raising duties well. The rest of life didn't seem to be going as smoothly. Sixth grade was harder than she had thought it would be. She missed her dad, and between school and homework and training classes and helping her mom with Will, it seemed to Caitlin that there wasn't much time to just hang out. Not that she had that many friends. She was still waiting to find the courage to talk to Shawna and some of the other girls in her class.

At least I talk to Keith every other week, she thought. *Too bad he goes to a different school.*

Inside the crowded mall, Caitlin stopped to take a picture of her mom and Will standing beside Alby.

"For the puppy book," she explained. "His first visit to the mall."

"Where are we going?" asked Will. "The toy store?"

"Actually," Kath replied, "I thought we would just walk around for a while. Let Alby get used to all the people and new smells and sounds. We have to keep exposing him to new situations so that nothing will surprise him when he's a working dog."

"Well, there are people and smells and sounds in the toy store," Will argued. "We could let him smell some action figures!"

"Good point." Kath laughed. "All right, let's head to the toy store."

"You take the leash, Mom," Caitlin urged. "I don't think I'm ready to handle Alby with all these people. It's not a puppy pile in here — it's a people pile."

Just then a little girl and her father walked by. The man was loaded down with shopping bags. His daughter, who looked about five, spotted Albion and grabbed her dad's hand.

"Daddy, look! A puppy! Can I pet him? Please?" she squealed. Her high-pitched voice instantly captured Alby's attention.

"Is that all right?" asked the man.

"Sure," said Kath, in a friendly but firm voice. "But you have to let me show you how, okay? He's in a special training program to teach him how to work with people in wheelchairs."

Kath put Alby in a sit position, then showed the

little girl how to pet him on top of his head. Alby sat for a moment, but then lurched forward to smell the girl's snow boots.

"Ah!" said Kath, correcting his behavior and giving the leash a tug. Alby quickly sat down again. "Good boy!" praised Kath.

"What a good dog," said the man. "My daughter doesn't even listen that well!"

Caitlin was proud of Alby. But she was also proud of her mom. She wondered if she would ever be able to act with such confidence, and to give instructions to total strangers.

An hour later, Kath and Caitlin could tell that both Alby and Will were growing tired of walking around. They had stopped at least a dozen times to explain to people why Alby was in the mall and why he was wearing a yellow cape.

And so far, Alby had barked at the indoor water fountain and at several strollers. Each time he saw something new, he acted just like a regular puppy. He either froze with fear or leaped forward to explore the new object. Caitlin thought he was cute when he barked at the fountain, but Kath made them take the time to let him get used to the sound of the rushing water and the smells around the fountain.

"Let's get some pizza for lunch," Kath suggested. "Alby can take a rest on the floor while we eat."

They entered a casual mall restaurant and were greeted by a man in a white apron, holding a pile of menus. He smiled at them and asked, "How many in your party?"

But the minute he spotted Alby, his smile disappeared.

"I'm sorry, but we can't allow dogs in here," he said. "It's against health regulations."

"This dog is in training to be an assistance dog," Kath explained patiently. "He has to accompany us to public places. Our state law allows it."

Caitlin took a deep breath, afraid of what was coming. This wasn't the first time they'd been questioned about Alby. She reached down and patted his head, proud of how quietly he sat. But she hoped the situation wouldn't become loud and embarrassing.

"I've never heard of any law like that," said the man. "I think you should leave before our customers start to complain."

"Caitlin," said Kath, "please let this gentleman see a copy of the law."

Caitlin unzipped her yellow pack and dug out a copy of the state law, which was printed on a small, plastic-coated card. She handed it to the man. Out of the corner of her eye, she suddenly noticed Shawna and her friends eating lunch at a nearby table.

This is all I need, she thought, discreetly unhooking the fanny pack and hiding it under her coat. *Let's just go home!*

The man glanced at the card without even reading it. Then he stared at Albion and Kath. "I'm sorry," he finally said. "But my manager's not here and I can't let you in with the dog."

"But it's the *law!*" shouted Will, who was

growing even more hungry and tired. "It says right there you have to let him in!"

Caitlin watched as Shawna turned to stare at Will. Caitlin's cheeks burned with embarrassment, and she wished the floor would open up and swallow her obnoxious little brother.

"Now, Will," said Kath, still using her patient voice, "we're not going to fight with this man."

"We're not?" Will asked. He sounded disappointed.

"No. We're going to have our organization write a letter to the manager and educate him on the law. And we're going to have our lunch some-where else."

Caitlin followed Kath and Alby out of the restaurant. She was afraid to turn around and see if Shawna was still watching them.

But even more than being embarrassed by the scene, she was angry at the man. *How could he be a grown-up and be so stupid? Why were people so ignorant about important laws like this?*

Everyone quickly agreed it was time to go

home. They were all tired from the eventful trip to the mall. And they decided it would be better to just warm up some soup and eat it in front of the fire. Caitlin settled Alby in his travel kennel in the back of the car, giving him a gentle kiss on the head.

"You were such a good boy," Caitlin said. But Alby was already asleep.

"He was great," Kath agreed. "Now that he's used to fountains, maybe we'll have some luck training him not to get distracted by birds and squirrels."

"You were great, too," said Caitlin. "I wish *I* could be so —"

"So mouthy?" Kath suggested. "Your brother and I are mouthy, aren't we? You're quiet, like your father."

Thinking about her father made Caitlin feel suddenly sad. She knew he was coming home in a few weeks for the holidays, but it would be hard to wait. Things just weren't the same without him. When he was gone, Caitlin felt she needed to act more grown-up and help her mom. She missed feeling like a little kid. She knew her mom was really lonely without her husband, and Will had been acting more and more like a kindergartner than a third-grader.

"You're not mouthy," Caitlin told her mom. "I think you're brave. I could never talk to people the way you do."

"Someday you will," her mom assured her.

But Caitlin wondered if it was true. She couldn't even talk to Shawna, who lived on her block and went to her school.

"Heeemm," sighed Alby in his sleep.

Caitlin peered into the kennel and watched as Alby's head and paws twitched. She knew he was having a dream. She loved the way he sometimes moved his legs wildly when he was fast asleep, probably dreaming of chasing squirrels.

"I love you," she whispered to Alby as the snow began to fall gently outside the car.

Alby's Puppy Book

December 10th

Well, the holidays are coming, so there are lots of new things for Alby to see and smell. We took him to the mall, which was really crowded, and he freaked out when he saw a guy dressed up as Santa Claus. But after he smelled the man's boots, he calmed down. Since Alby is still so young, we decided to get a very small Christmas tree and put it up on a table, so he won't be able to reach it and pull it over.

Alby wasn't sure what snow was the first time he saw it. He tried to eat it, then tried to get it off his paws. It was so cute! I found out that golden retrievers can stand really cold weather, though, because of their breeding and how thick their coats are. So, even when it's really cold and snowy out, Alby loves his walks. And I love to take him around our neighborhood. This is a map I drew of the route I follow when I walk Alby. We always end up at the park — his favorite place!

Well, whoever you are, I hope you have happy holidays, whichever ones you celebrate. By this time next year, you'll have Alby with you — won't that be a great present? He's getting so big now, you won't believe the next set of pictures.

January 1st

Happy New Year! Alby greeted the day by barking at some squirrels in our backyard. We're having to work really hard with him to curb this problem. Do you have squirrels where you live?

February 14th

Does it seem like I always write in this book on holidays? I guess since those are big days, they remind me to make an entry. My dad is home this weekend, so we took Alby to the movies. He was really good and slept at our feet. My dad also got to come with me to a training class and observe. It was fun to show him all the commands Alby has learned, and to intro—duce him to Bailey.

March 8th

My brother's Boy Scout troop had a meeting at our house. Will told the boys all about Alby and introduced him. Alby did really well around all the kids, until the troop leader started to demonstrate how to set up a tent in our living room. Well, since Alby had never seen a tent before, he was a bit alarmed at first. I had to help him approach it and not be afraid. Here's a picture of him finally sitting in the middle of the tent!

FOUR

Caitlin Takes the Leash

Boing, boing, boing.

Alby stood perfectly still as Regina Davis bounced a tennis ball up and down in front of his wet, black nose. It was a cool evening in May, and outside the rec center spring was in full bloom.

Boing, boing, boing.

You're doing great! thought Caitlin as she held Alby's leash in her hand. *What a good dog!* She understood what a challenge it was for any dog to resist wanting to play with a bouncing ball.

"Good boy!" Regina praised. She put the ball behind her back and smiled at Caitlin and Kath. "He did very well."

"I wish he would do as well around squirrels,"

sighed Kath. "He still barks sometimes when he sees them."

"That's a problem," Regina admitted. "Assistance dogs can't be distracted like that. How are you handling it?"

"We reward him every time he turns away from the squirrels and makes eye contact with one of us," Caitlin explained. "I think he's doing better."

"Sounds like you're doing the right thing," Regina said. But her voice sounded a tiny bit worried, Caitlin thought.

"Could barking at squirrels cause him not to graduate?" Caitlin asked.

"It could," admitted Regina, "if it remains a real problem. Remember, only fifty percent of the dogs in our program graduate — for all kinds of different reasons."

Caitlin looked down at Alby, still obediently sitting in his stay position. She felt extremely confused. On the one hand, she wanted him to graduate and show the world that he had been well loved and well trained. She wanted him to go on to become a companion to a disabled person and make that person's life better. But she also knew that if Alby *didn't* make it, her family would have the option of keeping him as a pet.

I would love to keep you forever, Caitlin thought, touching the soft underside of Alby's ear. *You're part of our family.*

Alby was ten months old now and looked more like the adult golden retrievers in the class. He had lost most of his puppy characteristics. Though he still had the same sweet face, to Caitlin he looked not just older, but smarter, too. His coat was sleek now, instead of fluffy, and the white fur on his chest and flanks added a handsome dignity. He had already grown through three different sizes of yellow capes!

"How are you doing?" asked Keith, coming over to join them with Bailey at his side. Bailey was nearly full-grown, too — a proud and striking animal, with a shiny ebony coat.

"We're talking about the squirrel problem," said Caitlin, rolling her eyes. "Alby can't keep his eyes off them. And he barks!"

"Don't feel bad," said Keith. "Bailey sometimes gets crazy when a flock of birds flies overhead."

"Really?" asked Caitlin.

"Well, you have to remember that retrievers were first bred to hunt birds. That was their main job in life."

"True," Regina agreed. "But Bailey's main job, we hope, will be to work with a disabled person. He can't take off, chasing ducks and geese, and leave his friend just sitting there."

"That wouldn't be good," Keith admitted. "You hear that, Bailey?" Bailey looked up at Keith, and his keen eyes seemed to say that he understood. "No more gawking at the geese!"

"Hey, I'm taking Alby to school on Friday," Caitlin said. "I mean, my mom and I are taking him. I have to give an oral report in social studies on something I've done to contribute to the community. It's our big project before the end of school."

"Cool!" said Keith. "Are you going to do all the talking? Or is your mom?"

"Caitlin is," said Kath. "It's her report. And she handles Alby very well now. I'm going to just sit very quietly in the back and try to be invisible."

"Are you ready to explain to your classmates how to behave around Alby?" asked Regina.

"I think so," Caitlin squeaked. "I mean, I am. I have to be."

"Just watch out for the jerks in your class," warned Keith.

"What do you mean?" asked Caitlin.

"Well, I took Bailey to school with my mom, and a few guys tried to give him food and stuff behind my back. I had to get right in their faces and tell them that he's not allowed to eat off the floor or from people's hands."

"What did they say?" Caitlin asked. The thought of a confrontation at school made her stomach feel queasy.

"They laughed at me. They were jerks. But I didn't care, because Bailey's future is my main worry. Right, boy?" Keith reached down to pet his dog's sturdy neck.

"Now you've made me nervous," said Caitlin. "I hate speaking in front of people, anyway. I've been practicing in front of my little brother. But he doesn't scare me the way some of the kids in my class do."

"You'll do great," Keith predicted.

"Just remember everything you've learned," added Regina. "Alby's a great dog."

"Yes, he is!" said Caitlin. She knelt down to stroke the white patch on his neck. "We're a team, aren't we, boy?"

Alby raised his ears and sat very still, as though he were practicing for his big debut at Caitlin's school.

On Friday morning, Caitlin felt sure she was losing her voice. She could barely swallow her cereal and juice.

Maybe I'm sick! Maybe I'm coming down with the flu and I won't have to go! she thought.

Caitlin reread the letter that had arrived from her father the day before, wishing her luck with her report. Caitlin couldn't believe that he had been gone for nine whole months. Though he had been home once or twice each month, his absence felt like a huge hole in the middle of her life.

"I miss Dad," croaked Caitlin. "I wish he were here. He always knows how to cheer me up with one of his stupid jokes."

"I'll tell you a stupid joke," offered Will. "Knock-knock."

"Who's there?" Caitlin responded, trying to clear her throat. "And this better be good."

"Boo."

"Boo who?" said Caitlin, playing along.

"Don't cry, it's only me!" Will shouted, cracking up at his own third-grade humor.

"Very funny," Caitlin said. "Shall I make you a peanut butter sandwich for lunch?"

"Stop it, you two," said Kath. She put her arm

around Caitlin's shoulder. "Honey, it's time to go. Alby's ready for his first day at school."

At Lincoln Middle School, the principal always greeted the students as they entered the main doors of the building each morning. She smiled broadly at Kath, Caitlin, and Alby.

"Good morning, Mrs. Spencer," Caitlin said shyly.

"Good morning," Kath added.

"Good morning!" Mrs. Spencer responded. "What a handsome dog. I hear you're giving a report about assistance dogs."

Caitlin nodded and looked down at Alby.

"I spoke with Ms. Tate," said Mrs. Spencer, "and we both agree that you should go directly to your social studies class and skip homeroom. That way you'll have time to get all set up before class."

"Thanks," Caitlin said. Then she led Alby and her mom down the long corridor to her social studies room. Ms. Tate got up from her desk the minute she saw them come in.

"Hello, Caitlin," she said in her friendly voice. "This must be your mom. And this must be Albion!"

Caitlin introduced everyone, and they chatted easily for fifteen minutes until the bell sounded for first period.

"Time to get started!" Ms. Tate exclaimed. "We have five reports today, and I've put you last, Caitlin, so that you'll have more time for questions. I'm sure the kids will have lots to ask you about!"

Caitlin and Kath took chairs in the back of the room, with Alby by their side. Caitlin took deep breaths to calm her racing heart.

When it was finally her turn, all eyes followed Caitlin as she took Alby's leash from her mom and led him up to the front of the class.

"Sit," she said.

Alby quickly sat, and a few kids called out their approval. Caitlin looked back at her mom, who gave her a thumbs-up for good luck.

Taking a deep breath, Caitlin glanced at her notes and then down at Alby.

Great, she thought. *If I look at Alby, I won't have to look at any of the other kids.*

"This is Albion," Caitlin began. "He's a ten-month-old golden retriever and he's in a special training program. Eventually, we hope he'll become an assistance dog for someone in a wheelchair."

The classroom became quiet as Caitlin continued her report. Though someone — Caitlin didn't see who — kicked a wadded-up piece of paper toward Albion near the end of the report, Alby didn't move a muscle.

I made it! thought Caitlin as she concluded her speech. *Now I just have to get through the question-and-answer portion.*

Caitlin took a deep breath and looked around. "Any questions?"

One of Shawna's friends, a girl with black hair and silver hoop earrings, raised her hand.

"Why do you have to wear that totally ugly yellow fanny pack?" asked the girl. Several students

laughed at the question, and Caitlin felt her cheeks flame.

"It's for carrying dog treats," Caitlin explained, "and a copy of the state law that gives us permission to enter public places with an animal." She struggled to keep her voice steady.

The next question was even worse! A tall boy who was on the basketball team asked how Albion could go to the bathroom when he was inside a mall or restaurant. The whole class burst out laughing.

"We teach them a command," explained Caitlin. "We take them outside and say, '*Better go now.*' The dogs learn to go, no matter where they are."

"What happens if you have a guest at your house and they accidentally say, '*Better go now*'?" asked the same boy, with a challenging grin.

Jerk! thought Caitlin.

"That's enough," said her teacher.

Finally, Caitlin noticed that Shawna had her hand raised.

"Yes?" said Caitlin. Her voice barely reached a whisper.

"Can I pet Albion?" Shawna asked.

Here goes, thought Caitlin.

"Yes, you can pet him, but you have to let me show you how."

Several students laughed again, and one of Shawna's friends quipped, "I think Shawna knows how to pet a dog. It's not brain surgery."

The class erupted in laughter again. But Shawna stood up and walked to the front of the room. Everyone quieted down.

"Sure," she said, her voice friendly. "Show me how to do it."

Caitlin put Alby in a sit position and began to explain that she couldn't allow the dog to lick, paw, or jump on anyone. "Because someday he'll have an important job to concentrate on," she said, "and he'll have to be focused and well behaved."

I did it! Caitlin thought. *I spoke up!*

She glanced at her mom, who was beaming

from the back of the room. Caitlin felt a rush of pride — for herself and for Alby.

Suddenly, Caitlin realized that she was standing in the center of a group of kids who were competing to talk to her and pet her dog. She was in the spotlight, for once in her life.

"Your dog is so cool," said Shawna. "And I think it's cool what you're doing. Can I come over and see him at your house?"

"Sure," said Caitlin, not quite believing her ears. "Come over after school sometime."

Caitlin knelt down and gave Alby a doggy treat from her fanny pack. "Good boy!" she whispered. "You deserve this. You just gave me one of the best days of my life."

Alby gave Caitlin his steady, devoted gaze, his chin tilted up, his eyes alert and curious.

To Caitlin, he seemed to be asking, "What now? What's my next assignment?"

Alby's Puppy Book

May 15th

Today was a really big "first" for Alby. He came to school with me and my mom because I gave an oral report on being a puppy raiser. He was the star of the class — everyone wanted to pet him and learn all about how he'll become an assistance dog. He was so well behaved. He kept in his "stay" even when a few kids tried to distract him.

But I must tell you that when he's just being a "regular" dog, he has developed quite a personality. Whenever I turn on some music and dance around, he comes running in with his doughnut in his mouth, shaking it back and forth. I think it's his way of dancing, too. And one day, my little brother and his friends had a parade outside with their bikes and wagons and Alby joined right in — holding his doughnut in his mouth!

Now that it's so warm outside, Alby is fascinated by blooming flowers and butterflies. Unfortunately, he still has a thing about squirrels — he loves to watch them, and some-times he barks at them. I promise we're still working really hard with him, but it's hard to get his attention away from those crazy squirrels.

July 4th

Another holiday entry! You can see by the pictures how big Alby is now. But he still has the same sweet face, don't you think? Yesterday, he got some burrs stuck in his coat and he was really patient while I took them out. In training class, we always spend time touching the dogs' paws, mouths, etc., so they won't have any sensitivity that could cause a problem later on. He even lets me brush his teeth — I never thought I'd brush a dog's teeth — and they're as white as when he was a tiny puppy.

I do wish I could see him swim sometime. Goldens love the water and have a natural instinct to swim, but we don't live near the water. Maybe YOU do, and you'll be able to see him swim — that would be cool!

FIVE

Birthday Blues

"Open *my* present next!" shouted Will.

He handed Caitlin a small square package wrapped in gold paper and tied with red and blue ribbons.

"Hey, thanks!" said Caitlin, removing a box of her very favorite chocolates. "These are the best! And I'll give all the ones with peanuts to you."

"That's the oldest joke in the world," Will replied, rolling his eyes. "You need some new jokes."

"And this gift is from Albion," said Kath, with a mysterious smile.

"Really? You remembered my birthday, Alby?" Caitlin leaned down and gave him a kiss on the nose. "What a good puppy!"

"He's not a puppy anymore," Will said.

"Don't remind me," answered Caitlin. "It's my birthday, and I don't want to think of anything depressing, like Alby getting any bigger and going away."

"We know it's coming, though," added Kath very gently. "Alby is already thirteen months old."

"That's almost seven in dog years!" said Will. "Me and Albion are almost the same age!"

Caitlin opened the slim package to find a picture of herself, standing next to Alby in training class. It was set in a silver frame, with the words FRIENDS FOREVER engraved on the bottom.

"This is great!" Caitlin exclaimed. "Alby, look. Here we are. What a team!"

Alby sniffed the picture and wagged his tail. Caitlin thought the photo perfectly captured Alby's attentive, intelligent expression.

"You could be in the movies," Caitlin told her dog. "You're so handsome."

"Just like Lassie," said Will.

"Thanks, Mom!" said Caitlin. "This is the best present."

"I just thought," explained Kath, "that it would be a good memento. I know that having a picture of Dad on my dresser has helped me not to miss him so much."

Caitlin knew her mom was trying to help her face the prospect of saying good-bye to Alby. Lately it seemed as if she brought it up in every conversation. But Caitlin somehow still believed that if she didn't talk about it, it might not happen.

"You know, Mom, Alby still barks at squirrels," Caitlin said softly. "Regina said that could be a real problem."

"That was months ago, honey. I haven't seen any of that behavior in a long time. Have you?"

"Well," Caitlin began, trying to remember. "Maybe not recently, but he could start up again at any time."

Kath looked as if she wanted to reply, but Will interrupted. "You still have one present left," he said. "Open it!"

"Who's it from?" Caitlin asked, examining the large, perfectly square box.

"Dad and me," said Kath, her eyes twinkling. "We had a lot of long-distance conversations about it."

"I can't believe Dad's not here for my birthday," sighed Caitlin. "It feels so weird without him."

"I know," Kath agreed. "He was really sad about not being here. But he'll soon be home for good."

Caitlin tore the paper from the box. "A bike helmet?" she asked, looking at the picture on the side.

"Yeah," said Will. "Mom told Dad that you have a really big head now."

"I did not!" Kath laughed. "I told him you had outgrown your old helmet. Look inside," she urged.

Caitlin opened the lid and took out a shiny silver-and-blue helmet. A small envelope was tucked inside.

"What's this?" she asked.

"The rest of the present."

Caitlin read the card out loud. "This certificate entitles Caitlin Connor to choose her own brand-new mountain bike. Happy Twelfth Birthday! Love, Mom and Dad."

"Oh, thanks!" Caitlin cried, jumping up to give her mom a hug. "It's the perfect present. My old bike does feel pretty small."

"I'm not sure who has grown faster this year," said her mom, "you or Alby. And I can't believe it's August and we all go back to school next month."

Just then the phone rang.

"It's probably Dad calling to say happy birthday," Kath said.

But after a few minutes, she returned to the dining room table with a strange expression on her face.

"Is it Dad?" Caitlin asked.

"Honey," Kath began, "I don't exactly know how to tell you this. It's bad timing, on your birthday and all —"

"What's the matter, Mom?"

"Caitlin, that was Regina."

"So?" Caitlin asked. "She calls all the time."

"We have to turn Alby in next month. They're ready for him to go to California and begin the next phase of his training."

Caitlin was stunned. She couldn't believe what she was hearing. "No!" she cried. "Already? It can't be!"

Kath moved to put her arms around her daughter. Alby, sensing a change of mood, stood up and put his head on Caitlin's knee.

"We always knew this call would come," her mom said, trying to soothe her daughter.

"But not so soon! Not on my birthday!" Hot tears began to trickle from Caitlin's eyes, and a sob caught in her throat. She bent down and wrapped her arms around Alby.

"I can't give you up," she said, burying her face in his fur.

Will moved over to pet Albion, too. With his other hand, he petted the top of his sister's head.

"It's okay," he said, and no one knew whether he was talking to Caitlin or the dog.

After a few minutes, Kath asked if anyone felt like having cake. "It's your favorite kind," she said. "Carrot cake with cream cheese frosting."

"I don't want cake," said Caitlin, standing up. "This is the worst birthday of my life!"

She ran from the room and bounded up the stairs. Alby immediately followed, leaving Kath and Will and a pile of torn birthday wrappings behind.

Later that evening, Caitlin and Albion finally emerged from Caitlin's room and came downstairs. Caitlin's eyes were swollen and red from crying, and her shirt was wrinkled and damp. She wandered into the kitchen, not sure what she was looking for. She felt hungry and sick at the same time.

The television was on in the family room, so Caitlin figured her mom and brother were watching a video. Her gifts were carefully stacked on the counter, including the framed picture of Caitlin and Alby.

"I should feed you, Alby," said Caitlin, looking at her watch. But then she spied her untouched birthday cake and stopped cold. An idea began to form and take hold.

Looking at Alby, Caitlin whispered, "Hey, you want to celebrate with me?"

Moving quickly, she took a knife from the drawer and cut a huge piece of cake. She centered it in the middle of a dinner plate and grabbed a fork.

"By my side," she said, and Albion hurried to stand next to her. Caitlin led him out the back door and onto the patio. She plopped down in a lawn chair. "Sit," she said, and Alby obeyed.

Then Caitlin ran a finger through the thick frosting and held it out for Alby to lick. He hesitated for a mere second before happily tasting the unexpected treat. Then Caitlin fed him a whole bite of cake. And then another. And another. Alby watched Caitlin's hand with intense concentration, waiting for the next taste of forbidden sugar.

"Honey, what are you doing?" asked Kath from the patio door. Her voice was sharp and it made Caitlin jump.

Caitlin turned to look at her mom, but didn't answer. Alby walked over and sniffed Kath's hand, as if he knew he was in trouble.

"Please tell me you weren't feeding cake to Alby," Kath said. "You know you're never supposed to do that."

Caitlin felt tears coming again. She couldn't make herself open her mouth to speak.

"Caitlin, you know he's not allowed people food!"

"I know!" Caitlin replied. Her tone was tense and angrier than she'd meant. "Don't you think I know that?"

"Then why did you do it? I don't understand."

Caitlin sniffed, trying to hold back the tears. "I don't know," she said. "I just thought — I thought that if Alby weren't such a good dog, and that if we relaxed the training a little bit, that maybe he —" Her voice cracked and she couldn't continue.

Gently, Kath finished her daughter's sentence. "You thought that maybe he wouldn't be good enough to graduate and we'd get to have him back?"

"Yes," admitted Caitlin. "Pretty stupid, huh?"

"Oh, honey, I know how you feel. I really do. Believe me, I've had those same thoughts."

"You have?" said Caitlin "You never told me."

"I guess I've tried to be strong for you. I've had to be both a mom and dad to you and Will this year, and I promised to be the primary puppy raiser for Alby. I had to keep my promise, no matter how hard it was.

"Oh, Mom," Caitlin began. She stood up and hugged her mom tight, resting her head on Kath's shoulder. "How are we going to say good-bye?"

"I don't know," Kath admitted. "I guess we'll have to make ourselves remember that Alby has a higher purpose to fulfill. I just keep thinking about someone, a child maybe, who can't use her arms or legs. And I think about Alby helping that person to get dressed and go places, the way Oz helps Mrs. Storbel at school —"

Kath stopped, tears filling her eyes, too.

"That's why you're the mom," Caitlin said. "Because you can be all wise and mature like that. Whenever I try to think about Alby leaving, I just feel sad for *me* instead of happy for someone else."

"That's why you're the kid," her mom joked, wiping her tears. "How about if we have some cake and sing to you? It won't feel like your birthday if you don't let us sing to you."

"I was such a jerk to feed Alby cake!" Caitlin said. "Do you think I ruined everything?"

"One mistake won't ruin all the months you've devoted to taking care of Alby," said her mom. "Don't be so hard on yourself."

Back inside, Will and Kath lit the candles and sang extra loud, to make up for their dad not being there.

As Caitlin blew out her candles, she still felt

torn between two different wishes. The little girl part of her still wished Alby never had to leave. But the twelve-year-old part of her wished for him to graduate and become the most amazingly devoted assistance dog in the world.

Alby's Puppy Book

August 2nd

Two big events this month: I turned twelve, and we got the call that Alby is going on to his advanced training program. I feel happy and sad at the same time. I know that in six months or so, Alby will be meeting you — whoever you are! Alby is now over a year old and fully grown, as you can tell from these recent pictures. Now when I go to training class and see the little puppies, I can barely remember Alby being that small.

With school out, I don't see a lot of kids my age, except for Keith. So, Alby is my main "buddy" in life. He still loves the park, though lately we've taken him to more and more different kinds of places, to get him used to life "on the go!" We even took him to an amusement park — talk about new sights and sounds! Think about what a roller coaster full of screaming people would sound like the first time you heard it. We also took him on a car trip to see my grandparents, who live on a very small farm where they grow organic herbs and a few vegetables. It's quiet there, but there are fun places to explore, like the woods and the tiny pond. Oh, yeah! I finally got to see Alby swim — here's a picture! He was great — just jumped in and started off. Not like me. I've had swimming lessons every summer of my

life, practically. He looked so cute when he got out — all wet
and shaggy. He shook himself dry about a hundred times and
then wanted to go back in.

August 20th

The vet says Alby is very healthy, and I'm including the
report from his last checkup. It tells his weight and even his
temperature — don't ask how they take a dog's temperature,
you don't want to know!

Believe it or not, Alby hasn't given up his chewy doughnut,
so you'll be getting that someday, along with this book. The toy
is a bit shabby by now, but he still loves to carry it around.

That's it for now. I'll try to take a lot of pictures this last
month. I hope you're having a good summer — whoever you are.

SIX

Saying Good-bye

Caitlin felt along the wall, trying not to bump into anything in the dark hall. When she reached Kath's bedroom, she paused in the doorway. She could see the outline of her mom, sleeping beneath the blue quilt. And next to the bed, Alby slept soundly in his crate. Caitlin could remember when Alby had been a puppy and they had put a cooler inside to make the crate more cozy. Now, his fully grown body took up the entire space!

Arranging her pillow and blanket on the nubby gray carpet, Caitlin snuggled down in front of the crate. Alby lifted his head to greet Caitlin but quickly returned to his slumber. Caitlin unlatched the door and reached inside to pet Alby's soft belly.

You're so warm, thought Caitlin. She kept her hand on Alby's side and tried to get comfortable.

"Who is it?" whispered Kath, suddenly awake but very groggy.

"It's me, Mom," Caitlin answered.

"What are you doing up, honey?"

"I couldn't sleep."

"Don't you feel well?"

"I'm not sick, if that's what you mean."

Kath leaned over the side of the bed and studied Caitlin and Alby. She suddenly understood what was going on — this was Alby's last night in the Connor home. In the morning, Regina would come to pick him up and prepare him for his flight back to California.

"Are you warm enough?" Kath asked. It was late September, and the nights had begun to turn chilly and damp.

"It's warm next to Alby," Caitlin whispered. "Do you think he knows about tomorrow?"

Kath considered the question. "I'm not sure,

Caitlin. We know dogs are very sensitive to changes in mood, but I don't think they have the ability to anticipate the future the way humans do."

"Do you think he'll remember us?" Caitlin asked.

"I like to think so," her mom answered. "I like to think that he'll carry us with him somehow."

"You know what I'll miss the most, Mom?"

"Tell me."

"The way he ran to the door every day when I got home from school — as if just seeing me was the best part of his day."

"I think I'll miss having him curled up at my feet whenever I'm using the computer or reading," said Kath. "And watching him learn new things in training class."

"I'll miss seeing him march around the house with his squeaky doughnut in his mouth," Caitlin said, laughing. She stroked Alby's neck and rubbed his ears. He gave a sleepy sigh and turned to his other side.

"Do I have to go to school tomorrow?" Caitlin asked.

"Yes," said Kath. "You've just begun a new school year — you can't miss class so early in the term."

"I can't believe that Alby came to us almost exactly a year ago," mused Caitlin. "Having Dad away has gone so slowly. But raising Alby has gone so fast!"

"I know what you mean." Kath yawned. "We should get some sleep."

"Mom?" said Caitlin. She felt tears spilling down her cheek.

"Hmm?"

"I don't think I can say good-bye in the morning."

"However you want to handle it, honey," Kath said. "If you want to sleep next to him and let that be your good-bye — then it's fine with me."

"You'll give Regina the puppy book and the squeaky doughnut?"

"I won't forget," her mother answered.

Caitlin moved her hand so it rested on Alby's front paw. His breathing was slow and relaxed, yet Caitlin knew that if she gave a command, he would instantly respond. She tried to picture Alby lying beside a different bed, ready to be a helpful companion to someone who spent her daylight hours in a wheelchair.

The thought comforted Caitlin, but still the tears snaked down her cheeks.

"I'll love you forever," she whispered to Alby. "You've been the best thing in my life. And I'll never forget you. Good-bye, sweet boy."

Alby nuzzled Caitlin's hand, and she knew inside her heart that he, too, was saying good-bye.

Albion's Puppy Book

September 30th

I can't believe it, but this is my very last entry in this book.
Tomorrow Alby goes on a jet to California. Regina will pick him up
and take him to the airport in a travel kennel — not the one he
came in, because he's huge now. Mom and I decided it would
be too hard to go to the airport, so we're all saying good-bye
tonight.

This last picture is of the puppy raisers' luncheon where
we were honored for the time spent raising our dogs. It was
fun — we all got to stand up with our dogs and everyone
clapped for us. Then we had lunch and watched a slide show
about the next phase of training. They also showed a graduation. It made me cry, and made me hope more than ever that
Alby passes his next six months of training.

I've never had anyone I loved go away, except for my best
friend in first grade and my dad this past year. So I'm not
really sure how to handle this. I don't know what Alby will think
when Regina takes him away. I'm trying to think about you —
whoever you are — and how happy you'll be to have Alby for
your companion. Maybe we'll get to meet someday — maybe at
the graduation. I hope this isn't too dumb to say, but I'm sorry

for whatever caused you to be in a wheelchair. And I hope Alby makes your life so much happier and easier. He sure made mine happy. I call our year together "the golden year" — you can guess why.

Please, please take good care of my dog — I mean YOUR dog. And I hope you enjoy this scrapbook of Alby. He's the best dog in the world. Soon you'll know that for yourself.

Sincerely,
Caitlin Marie Connor
Puppy Raiser

SEVEN

Life After Alby

"I dream about Alby all the time," Caitlin said.

"Me too, about Bailey," admitted Keith. "But don't tell anyone. People would think we were really weird if they knew we dreamed about our dogs."

"And they're not even our dogs anymore." Caitlin sighed.

The two friends were sitting on Caitlin's front porch. It was a Saturday afternoon in mid-October, and Keith had ridden his bike over to visit. Yellow leaves rained down from the huge elm tree in Caitlin's front yard, covering the grass beneath it.

Ever since Keith and Caitlin had turned in their dogs, they'd been spending more and more time

together. No one else seemed to understand what they were going through. The loss they each felt strengthened and deepened their friendship.

"I wonder how they're doing in their training," mused Caitlin.

"At least we'll get a call every month for the next six months, telling us how things are going," said Keith. "I can't wait for the first call."

"Me too," Caitlin said. "Every time the phone rings, I jump. I think it'll be Regina, telling me that Alby still barks at squirrels. Or that he can't learn the new commands."

"Think about all the new stuff they must be learning," said Keith. "Opening doors and turning on televisions and pulling socks out of a drawer!"

Just then, Caitlin spotted Shawna riding up the street on her bike. Caitlin was surprised to see that, for once, Shawna wasn't surrounded by a group of laughing friends. But she was even more surprised when Shawna stopped in front of Caitlin's house.

"Hi!" said Shawna, smiling and waving.

"Hi, Shawna. What's up?" asked Caitlin.

"Just thought I'd say hello."

Caitlin introduced Keith to Shawna, and explained how they had met in puppy-training class.

"I heard you had to give your dog back," Shawna said. "You must really miss him."

"I do," said Caitlin. "And Keith misses Bailey. So we're just sitting around feeling miserable."

"I'm sorry," said Shawna. "That was really neat when you brought Alby to school last spring."

She sounded very sincere to Caitlin. And she seemed different than when she was with her friends.

"Where are all your friends?" asked Caitlin, trying to sound casual.

"I don't know." Shawna shrugged. "Everything seems really different this year. Maybe it's me, but the friend thing has been pretty weird. And my parents are separating, so I've been spending a lot of weekends with my dad."

"Wow. I'm sorry," Caitlin said. "I think I know

how you feel. My dad's been working in another state for a whole year. And my mom has gone back to teaching, after a year off. It's definitely weird."

"Maybe the planets are in some strange alignment," Keith said. "Maybe the moon is in Venus or something."

Suddenly Will came running from the backyard, crying hard and holding his hand.

"What's wrong, buddy?" Keith asked, hurrying to meet him.

Between sobs, Will explained that he had hit his hand with a hammer. "I'm tired of trying to build my fort all alone. I started it with Dad, and I want to finish it, but it's turning out awful!"

"Dad will be back next week — for good," Caitlin said, ruffling her brother's red hair, which was now flecked with sawdust. "Then you'll have some help again."

"Hey," said Keith, "maybe we could help you out. We're just sitting around feeling sorry for ourselves, talking about Alby and Bailey."

"Yeah," added Caitlin. "It might make us forget about our problems."

"Great!" said Will, drying his eyes. "That would be great!"

"Um, do you think I could help, too?" Shawna asked softly — almost shyly. "I'm pretty good with a hammer."

Caitlin smiled at Shawna, painfully aware of how hard it was to try to be included in a group. "Sure," she said. "The more the merrier. I'll go get some drinks and snacks. Peanuts for you, Will."

"That's so funny I forgot to laugh," screamed Will.

"Private joke," Caitlin explained to her friends, winking at Will.

Life is so strange, thought Caitlin as she went inside the house. *I had to give up my dog, but I have two new friends! And a golden retriever brought us all together!*

EIGHT

It's a Go!

"Look outside!" shouted Will. "It's snowing so hard my fort is almost covered."

Caitlin and her dad, Ned, looked up from the chocolate chip cookies they were baking and watched the snow fall outside the kitchen window.

"Looks like quite a storm," said Ned. "We'll have a white Valentine's Day for sure."

Caitlin put another tray of cookies in the oven and set the timer. It felt so nice to be in the warm kitchen with her dad and brother, surrounded by the aroma of freshly baked cookies. Though her father had been home since right before Halloween, Caitlin still felt an extra surge of happiness whenever she spent time with him.

"You should have seen Alby the first time it snowed," Caitlin remembered.

"What did he think of it?" asked Ned.

"He couldn't figure out what it was. The minute we took him outside, he started sniffing the snow like crazy. Then his face got covered and he had to shake his head. Then he tried walking in the snow, and it must have felt weird because he was doing this little dance, hopping up and down."

"I bet he never sees snow in California," said Will. "I wonder if he ever sees the ocean."

"You're still missing him, aren't you?" asked Ned. He put his arm around Caitlin's shoulders and gave her a squeeze.

"Everything reminds me of him," Caitlin admitted. "The first time he saw snow, the first time he saw a fountain, the way he was afraid of the ironing board the first time he ever saw it."

"And the way he barked at squirrels," added Will.

"Let's hope he doesn't do that anymore," said

Caitlin. "Someone would have told us during one of the monthly calls."

"From all reports," said Ned, "it sounds as if Alby is doing really well in his training."

"He is," Caitlin agreed. "But you never know. Something could happen at the last minute."

"Time's almost up," said Will.

"Don't remind me," Caitlin said flatly.

"I meant the cookies, not Alby," Will explained.

Caitlin took the cookies out of the oven and placed them on top of the stove to cool. Ned and Will both reached for a hot cookie at the same time.

"Do you sometimes still hope that Alby doesn't graduate?" Ned asked, between bites of cookie.

Caitlin took a cookie and blew on it. She thought about her dad's question. "Not so much anymore," she answered finally. "I mean, a tiny part of me still dreams about that, but mostly I want him to graduate. It wouldn't seem right for him to have worked so hard and come so far, only to fail at the end."

"That's a very mature attitude," Ned remarked. "Did you know your mom is considering raising another puppy?"

"She told me," said Caitlin.

"How do you feel about that?"

"I think it would be cool!" said Will. "And, Dad, you'd be here to help us this time."

"Sometimes I think it would be great," Caitlin said. "But then sometimes I think it would be hard to love another dog the way I loved Alby. No other dog could take his place."

"Well, we don't have to decide right now," Ned said. "Let's wait and hear about Alby."

"We should hear any time now," said Caitlin. "Every time the phone rings I jump."

"I talked to Mom, Caitlin," Ned said. "And we decided that if Alby graduates, Will and I will stay here and you and Mom can fly to California."

"We can? That's great! I've never been to California."

"Why can't we go, too, Dad?" Will pouted. "Caitlin gets to have all the fun."

"We can't afford for all of us to go," Ned explained. "Since Caitlin and Mom were the official raisers, it seems only fair that they go out there and see this project through to the end."

As Ned and Caitlin washed the dishes, Kath wandered into the kitchen, wrapped in a sweater. She helped herself to a cookie and said, "I was grading papers, but this incredible smell from downstairs kept distracting me."

The phone rang, and Kath hurried to swallow her cookie so she could answer it. Caitlin studied the swirl of snowflakes pasted on the kitchen window.

"Caitlin, it's for you," she heard her mother say.

"It's probably her lover boy, Keith-y!" taunted Will, stealing one last cookie.

"He's not my lover boy!" Caitlin said with a sigh, wiping her soapy hands on a towel. "He's my *friend*. But you're too immature to understand the concept, so go eat a peanut. I should have made peanut butter cookies instead of chocolate chip!"

Taking the phone, Caitlin watched to make

sure that Will was gone. He loved to hang around whenever she talked to Shawna or Keith and repeat every single word she said in a high, whiny voice.

"Hello?" she said when the coast was clear.

"Hey, Caitlin, it's Regina."

Caitlin's heart began to pound. "Hi, Regina."

"Are you sitting down?"

"Why?"

"Because I have some pretty amazing news."

"You do?"

"It's a go! Alby's going to graduate. We just got word."

"He is?" Caitlin could hardly get her voice above a whisper. It felt as if her stomach were dropping down to her feet — like the moment when the roller coaster begins to plunge downhill.

"He passed with flying colors. You should be very proud," Regina continued.

"I can't believe it," Caitlin answered. "Wait one second."

Caitlin covered the phone with her hand and

called for her parents and Will. Something in the sound of her voice brought them running.

"Alby's going to graduate!" she announced, a huge smile replacing her shocked expression.

Shouts, whistles, and applause followed her big news. Kath hugged her daughter, practically jumping up and down. Will did a somersault right on the kitchen floor, and Ned took Caitlin's hand and gave her an exaggerated handshake of congratulations.

Back on the phone, Caitlin asked the question most on her mind. "Who was Alby matched with?"

"He's been matched with a girl about your age. From Oregon. She has a disease called muscular dystrophy."

"Wow," Caitlin breathed. "Does she — like Alby?"

"Caitlin, she's thrilled with Albion. They're a wonderful match. Are you coming for graduation?"

"My mom and I are planning to be there."

"Great. You can meet her then. Her name is Jessica, and she's really excited about meeting you."

Caitlin tried to imagine what Jessica might look like. And what Alby would look like standing by her wheelchair. She had to admit that while she was happy and excited, she also felt a pang of jealousy. It was hard to think of her dog — no, not her dog — of Alby lovingly attached to someone new.

"You still there?" asked Regina.

"Sorry," said Caitlin. "I was just thinking."

"It's big news to digest," Regina agreed. "I hope you know how proud we are of you, here at the agency. And how grateful we are for all you've done to help us."

"Thank you," Caitlin answered. "I feel — well, I feel a lot of different things."

"That's natural," said Regina. "So, we'll see you in California next month?"

"Yes. Oh, and Regina? Before I forget — did Bailey make it, too?"

There was a brief silence from Regina. Then

she cleared her throat. "I just talked to Keith and his family. Bailey has developed a hip problem. He won't be graduating."

No! thought Caitlin. *It can't be. It's not fair! Keith will be so sad!*

"Caitlin?" said Regina. "It's okay. Keith is disappointed, but there's a happy ending. Bailey's coming back to live with them."

After Caitlin and Regina said good-bye, Caitlin hung up the phone and leaned against the wall.

"What's the matter?" asked Kath. "Is it about Bailey?"

"He's not going to graduate. Something's wrong with his hips."

"Oh, honey. I'm so sorry! Do you want to call Keith?"

"Yes. But I don't know what to say."

"It's a tough situation," Kath agreed. "But I know he'll appreciate your friendship right now."

Caitlin turned and picked up the phone. *Here goes,* she thought.

"And when you're finished," Kath continued,

"I'll call the airlines and make our reservations for California."

As Caitlin dialed Keith's number she thought, *Why does it always seem as if good news and bad news come so close together? Alby graduates and Bailey doesn't. Jessica will have Alby now, and I won't. Bailey will live with Keith, and I'll never see Alby again.*

NINE

Graduation Day

"I can't believe how nervous I am!" Caitlin told her mom. She tucked her purple shirt back into her new black jeans for about the twentieth time since lunch.

"Me too," said Kath. "I hardly slept last night, even though the hotel room was so quiet."

"What time is it?" Caitlin asked. She looked around the empty hotel meeting room for a clock, but couldn't find one.

"One-thirty, California time," Kath said, checking her watch. "Which means it's already four-thirty in the afternoon back home."

"I wonder what Dad and Will are doing right now?" Caitlin said. "I wish they could have come for the graduation."

"They're probably riding bikes. The weather has been so beautiful for early March."

Just then the door to the room edged open and Caitlin caught sight of a wet black dog nose.

"Alby!" she cried, running for the door.

"Hi," said an older man with white hair. "I'm Steve, and I'm a volunteer with Canine Family." He held Alby's leash out to Caitlin. "I think this is an old friend of yours."

Caitlin knelt down beside Alby, marveling at how grown-up he looked. Alby immediately sniffed her hand and looked up at Caitlin with his familiar brown eyes.

"Do you think he remembers us?" Caitlin asked.

"Sure he does," the man answered. "You were his first family."

Kath came over and patted Alby on his soft golden head, already blinking back a few tears. "Hey there, Alby. How are you? You look just great."

"He does," Caitlin agreed. Obviously, he had been well cared for during the past several months.

His coat was clean and shiny, his eyes alert, and his teeth as white as when he was a puppy. He wagged his tail happily as Caitlin petted him.

"I'll leave you for a few minutes," said the volunteer. "But I need to come back for him soon. It's just about time for the big moment." He stepped out of the room, closing the door behind him.

Alby, in his sit position, seemed calm and content. He watched Caitlin and Kath closely, but made no move to jump or play. Caitlin studied him, then looked up at her mom.

"Doesn't he already seem a little different?" she asked.

"How do you mean?"

"I don't know. Very . . . settled. Like he's already a working dog."

"As of today, he is," said Kath. "He starts a whole new life. And so does Jessica."

"I'm so nervous about meeting her," Caitlin confessed. "I wish I could have met her before the ceremony."

"Well, we'll have lots of time to talk with her at

the party afterward," Kath said consolingly. "I bet she's nervous about meeting you, too."

Caitlin picked up Alby's front left paw and examined his pads and nails. "Look how nice your paws look," she said. "Regina would be proud." Caitlin remembered how often Regina had reminded the puppy raisers to take extra care of their dog's paws.

"How about if I leave you and Alby alone to say your last good-bye?" Kath suggested.

Caitlin nodded, afraid her voice would give away her growing emotion.

Kath slipped out, and Caitlin knew she had only a moment or two left with Alby.

"Hey," she said, putting on a brave smile, "I have an idea. I could just take you by the leash and run out the door! We could keep on going and never look back."

Alby cocked his head to one side and looked at Caitlin, as if trying to make sense of her words. Caitlin had promised herself she wouldn't cry, so she tried to make another joke.

"Maybe," she began with a little half laugh, "you could do something really terrible, just at the last minute, and you wouldn't graduate. Like, maybe you could bite Jessica. Or bite me! Go ahead, I'll let you! I won't hold it against you. Then you can come home on the plane with me and visit your old pal, Bailey. He's back home waiting for you."

But no matter how light Caitlin tried to keep her voice, and how silly she tried to sound, her heart felt as if it were cracking. A few tears escaped, and rolled down her cheeks. She wiped them away, knowing she had to take this final step and say good-bye to her friend.

"We have to say good-bye, Alby," she whispered. "You have a whole new life waiting for you — right outside that door. And you and Jessica are going to be a great team. You taught me a lot — like how to speak up for myself. And how to take good care of an animal —"

The door opened and Caitlin pressed her face against Alby. Kath joined her daughter as the Canine Family volunteer took Alby by the leash.

"Are you ready?" he asked. "I'll lead Alby into the auditorium, and then you'll wait in the back to present him to his new partner."

"Ready as I'll ever be," sighed Caitlin. She followed her mom, the volunteer, and the beautiful golden retriever to the graduation ceremony.

Caitlin scanned the people on the stage, trying to pick out Jessica. It wasn't too hard, because she was the only young girl in the line of twelve people in wheelchairs. She had long blonde hair woven into a complicated French braid. Her dress was a gauzy blue and green. To Caitlin, it looked like pictures of Earth from outer space.

She looks nice, Caitlin thought. *And I think she's as excited as I am.*

Finally, it was Caitlin's turn. The woman at the microphone said, "And now I'd like you to meet Caitlin Connor, who was a co-raiser with her mother, Kath Connor. Caitlin and Kath gave a year of their lives to raise Albion, who has been matched with Jessica Stern. Caitlin, would you come forward, please?"

As Caitlin stepped forward, Alby at her side, her heart pounded inside her chest. The crowd applauded for both of them as they made their way to the stage. For once, Caitlin didn't blush and lower her eyes. She looked ahead, right at Jessica, proud to be presenting her with such an incredible dog.

As Caitlin approached, Jessica reached for the leash. Caitlin handed it over to her, and Alby went immediately to Jessica's side. Jessica patted Alby's head and whispered, "Good boy!"

Then Jessica reached forward to hug Caitlin, and Caitlin leaned down to embrace Alby's new partner. Jessica had tears in her eyes, and so did Caitlin.

"Thank you!" said Jessica. "Thank you so much!"

"You look good together," Caitlin whispered. "You look like you belong together."

* * *

Later, at the reception, Caitlin and Jessica had another chance to talk as they each ate a piece of the huge cake decorated with dozens of dogs made of frosting. Albion sat next to Jessica, not even tempted by all the food around him.

"One time," Caitlin confided, "I fed Alby some of my birthday cake. I knew I wasn't supposed to, but I thought it would mess up his training and I'd get to keep him."

"It must be really hard to give him up," said Jessica. "I feel so attached to him already, and we've only been working together for a few weeks."

"It *is* sad," Caitlin admitted. "But meeting you makes it so much better. I know he's going to be with people who love him."

"We do," Jessica said. "My parents are crazy about him. I want you to meet them — if I ever find them in this crowd."

"Can you go out alone with Albion," Caitlin asked, "or do you have to have an adult with you?"

"For now," Jessica explained, "I have to have

Mom or Dad with me. It will be a while before we can go it alone. Right, Alby?"

Alby looked at Jessica with utter devotion in his eyes. Caitlin could only imagine the kinds of adventures the two of them would have together.

"You must have had to learn a ton of commands," said Caitlin, remembering when Alby was just learning to sit and stay.

"About a thousand." Jessica laughed. "Watch this. I'll show you one."

As Caitlin stared in amazement, Jessica commanded Alby to stay by her side as she navigated her chair toward a door. When they reached the door, she asked Alby to open it for her — and Alby did!

"Wow!" Caitlin sputtered. "That was great!"

"My arms get weak sometimes, so having Alby do things like that for me will really make life easier."

"Aren't goldens amazing?" said Caitlin. "I still can't believe how smart they are."

"And how loving," Jessica added. "Thanks for

loving him so much. That's what makes him able to love me. I'll never forget you."

"Thanks," Caitlin replied. "I'll never forget you, or Alby, or this entire day."

"Hey," said Jessica, "if you'll give me your address, I'll send you some pictures. And I'll let you know how he's doing."

"I would really love that," Caitlin said with a smile. "May I ask you a question?"

"Sure."

"Does he ever bark at squirrels?"

Jessica thought for a minute. "It's never happened that I know of. Why?"

"No reason." Caitlin laughed. "I was just wondering."

Then Caitlin looked around the crowded room for her mom. She was suddenly tired — worn out from the emotion of the day.

Her job was finished. She was ready to go home.

A New Beginning

"Look," Keith said. "A daffodil coming up through the snow. This has been a spring of wild weather!"

Sure enough, Caitlin could see a tiny yellow shoot peeking out of a crusty patch of ice by the south side of her front porch.

"Go figure." She laughed. "Snow and blooming flowers, both in April."

It made her think again about all the difficult things that happened in life, and how they could be so closely followed by wonderful things. It made her think about missing Alby, and yet how happy she was at the moment. Her father didn't have to work in another city, she had Keith and Shawna for friends, and spring was definitely coming. Soon she could ride her bike again, and wear shorts to school!

"Bailey, come!" shouted Keith.

Caitlin looked up to see Bailey nosing under the spruce tree for pinecones. When the dog heard Keith's voice, he turned and ran to the porch. He was panting heavily, and his thick black tail swished back and forth. Sitting calmly by Keith's side, he suddenly spotted a flock of geese flying overhead. Instantly alert, Bailey watched the birds with every cell in his body.

"It's a good thing he didn't graduate," said Keith. "He still gets distracted by birds."

"But he doesn't bark," Caitlin answered.

"True," Keith admitted, giving Bailey a pat on the side. "He's a pretty well-trained dog."

"He should be, after all your hard work. He's a great dog!"

"Thanks," said Keith, smiling at the compliment.

"I still miss Alby," Caitlin admitted.

"I bet you always will. But it will get easier as

time goes by, don't you think?" Keith asked.

Caitlin nodded her head. "And Jessica said she'll send me pictures and letters. So I have that to look forward to."

The two friends were quiet for a minute, watching Bailey lick his enormous paws.

"When do you think you'll hear from her?" Keith asked.

"I don't know," said Caitlin. "She has my address. But Regina said it may be a while — they need time to settle in together."

"Hey," said Keith, "maybe she'll call and tell you it's not working out between the two of them."

"Probably not," sighed Caitlin.

"Probably not," Keith agreed. "Want to take a walk with me and Bailey?"

"Sure," said Caitlin, standing up and dusting off her jeans.

They took off down the street, Bailey walking easily by Keith's side. Caitlin wished she had Alby beside her, his tags clinking together as they explored the neighborhood.

A few snowflakes fell softly around them — fat spring flakes that melted before they hit the ground.

"Guess what?" Keith said to Caitlin as they rounded the corner at the end of the street.

"What?"

"You're not going to believe it."

"Tell me," Caitlin urged.

"Well, we're actually thinking about being puppy raisers again."

Caitlin froze in her tracks and turned to look at Keith. "You're kidding?" she said. "Really?"

"Really. We must be crazy!"

Caitlin started to laugh, her breath coming out in cold puffs. "Guess what?"

"What?"

"So are we!"

"You are?" shouted Keith. "Yes!"

He turned to Caitlin and gave her a high five.

Bailey, trying to understand the happy shouts, walked around them, tangling up his leash.

"Power to the puppy raisers!" Keith hollered, straightening out the leash and taking off in a run.

"Power to the puppy raisers!" Caitlin shouted, running to catch up. "And power to the puppies!"

Golden Retriever Facts

1. Goldens were first bred by an Englishman named Lord Tweedmouth, in the mid-nineteenth century. They are thought to be a cross between the flat-coated retriever, the bloodhound, and the water spaniel.

2. Golden retrievers were officially recognized as a distinct breed in 1913 in Great Britain, and in 1925 in the United States.

3. Goldens are the perfect family pet because they are calm, gentle, loyal, and very loving toward humans.

4. Because of their intelligence, goldens are also ideal as working or assistance dogs. They have

the ability to learn and remember many commands and are quite easy to train.

5. Goldens were first bred as hunting dogs. Because of their ability to withstand cold weather and their love of water, they are well suited to leaping into ponds and retrieving waterfowl.

6. Goldens also have a highly developed sense of smell and are natural trackers.

7. Physically, goldens are sturdy, well-built dogs with wavy golden or cream-colored coats. Their coats are dense and waterproof. The adult dog weighs up to 65 or 75 pounds, and stands 20 to 24 inches tall.

8. Goldens have black noses, wide-set brown eyes with brown rims, and strong jaws with a scissor bite. Their tails are carried level with the back of the dog and do not curl up at the end.

9. Golden retrievers love to be around people, and do not do well when left alone for long periods

of time. Because they are sporting dogs, they need plenty of exercise every day.

These dog facts were compiled from the following sources:

The Reader's Digest Illustrated Book of Dogs. Pleasantville, NY: The Reader's Digest Association, Inc., 1993.

Casanova, Mary. *The Golden Retriever.* New York: Crestwood House, 1990.

Taylor, David. *The Ultimate Dog Book.* New York: Simon and Schuster, 1990.

About the Author

Growing up in Denver, Colorado, Coleen Hubbard liked to write and put on plays in her backyard. As an adult, she still writes plays. She also now writes for children and young adults. Among her works are four books in the Treasured Horses series, which sparked her interest in writing fun books about animals and kids.

Coleen and her husband have three dog-crazy young daughters, plus Maggie the Magnificent, a sweet-natured mixed breed who inspired Coleen to learn all about the various breeds of dogs featured in the Dog Tales series.